Under Threat

Under Threat

Robin Stevenson

ORCA BOOK PUBLISHERS

Library and Archives Canada Cataloguing in Publication

Stevenson, Robin, 1968–, author
Under threat / Robin Stevenson.
(Orca soundings)

Issued in print and electronic formats.
ISBN 978-1-4598-1131-7 (paperback).—ISBN 978-1-4598-1132-4 (pdf).—
ISBN 978-1-4598-1133-1 (epub)

I. Title. II. Series: Orca soundings
PS8637.T487U54 2016   jc813'.6   C2015-904492-8
C2015-904493-6

First published in the United States, 2016
Library of Congress Control Number: 2015946329

Summary: In this high-interest novel for teen readers, a girl struggles with the threats
her abortion-providing parents are receiving and the reactions of her girlfriend's family.

*Orca Book Publishers is dedicated to preserving the environment and has
printed this book on Forest Stewardship Council® certified paper.*

Orca Book Publishers gratefully acknowledges the support for its publishing programs
provided by the following agencies: the Government of Canada through the Canada
Book Fund and the Canada Council for the Arts, and the Province of British Columbia
through the BC Arts Council and the Book Publishing Tax Credit.

Cover image by iStock.com

ORCA BOOK PUBLISHERS
www.orcabook.com

Printed and bound in Canada.

19 18 17 16 • 4 3 2 1

To all the dedicated and courageous individuals who fight to keep abortion safe, legal and accessible.

Chapter One

"So did you ride after school? How is that horse of yours?" Dad asks me.

We're eating dinner, which I made— chicken with feta cheese and green peas on linguine. Learning to cook was one of my New Year's resolutions. "He's doing well," I say. "Walking and trotting without a limp. I'm taking it slow with him though. Letting that tendon heal."

"Well, it was just as well you decided to retire from jumping when you did," Mom says. She points at her dinner plate with her fork. "Franny, this is delish."

"Don't know where she got it from, but our girl can cook," Dad says approvingly. "This recipe is definitely a keeper."

"Good. Glad you like it." I'm not surprised he does—the dish is way too salty, which is exactly what his blood pressure doesn't need. I'd forgotten how high in sodium feta is. "I wouldn't have had time to show this year anyway," I say, twirling my fork on the pasta. "Even if Buddy wasn't lame. The amount of homework I have is insane."

"Not to mention your love life," Dad says, rolling his eyes. "Every time I see you, you're texting your girlfriend." He's grinning though. He adores Leah. He and Mom both do.

"What bothers me," Dad says, "is that your horse got to retire before I did. I mean, I'm pushing seventy."

"Sixty-seven," I correct him quickly. He's ten years older than mom, and she was forty when I was born, so they are kind of old for parents. But *seventy*? That's well into grandparent age.

"And Buddy is still in his teens."

"Almost twenty," I say. "Which is getting on for a horse."

Dad ignores me. "And he has a sore ankle. I had a stroke! Shouldn't that trump a sore ankle?"

"Sore *fetlock*," I say, even though I know he's well aware that horses don't have ankles. "And you didn't have a stroke, Dad. You had a transient ischemic attack. Which isn't a real stroke. Just a warning." What I don't say is that a third of people who have a TIA go on to have a stroke within a year. He's well aware of that too.

"Who's the doctor here?" he says.

And then the phone rings. I start to get up, even though Leah doesn't usually use the landline, but Dad waves a hand at me. "Let the machine get it. Neither of us is on call."

I sit back down, twirl a fork full of linguine and chew slowly. Definitely too much salt. Not good, considering the only reason I took over the cooking was to stop the family reliance on takeout and make sure Dad ate healthier meals.

The phone rings and rings. Let it be Leah, I think, let it be Leah. I picture her face—her blue-green eyes, her silky brown hair, the deep dimples that appear when she smiles, the way she covers her mouth with her hand when she laughs.

I was just with her, but I miss her already.

Leah's family owns the farm where I keep Buddy now. Gibson's Farm— or Buddy's Retirement Home, as Dad calls it. I was heartbroken when Buddy developed a limp right at the start of last show season, but if he'd stayed sound, and we'd kept jumping and competing, I'd probably never have met Leah Gibson. So that's kind of a crazy thought. We've only been together for a few months, but I've never felt like this about any other girl.

No matter how much time I spend with Leah, it's not nearly enough. Even when I'm with her, I sometimes feel this ache, like I can't get close enough, can't hold her tight enough, can't kiss her long enough. I've had other girlfriends, but I've never felt like this before.

It's crazy and, to be honest, a little scary.

Just two hours ago, we were sitting on a bale of hay outside the tack room, cleaning the school horse bridles and listening to the horses munch their oats. Leah's brother, Jake, was teaching a private lesson in the arena, and I could hear his voice—"Extended trot doesn't mean go faster, Brandy! I want to see longer strides, not speed! Contain that energy!" It was like listening to the soundtrack of my childhood. Leah turned to me and said, "I love the sound of horses eating."

I love you, I thought. I love you.

We hadn't said those words yet, but I thought them the whole time I was with her—and most of the time I wasn't with her too.

The machine beeps and picks up. "You've reached the home of Heather, Hugh and Franny Green. Leave a message and one of us will get back to you."

I stop chewing for a second, listening, in case it's for me. But it's a man's voice, deep and oddly muffled. "Baby killers," he says. "You're going to burn in hell for what you do." *Click.*

My heart flip-flops in my chest, and my cheeks flare hot.

Mom sighs. "So much for changing the number and having it unlisted," she says. "How long did it take for them to get the new one?"

Dad runs his hands over his bald head. "Not nearly long enough."

The phone starts to ring again.

"Unplug it, would you, Franny?" Mom says. Her voice is calm, as always. She's the most level-headed, unflappable person I've ever met.

"We'll have to change the number again," Dad says.

"We should just get rid of the land-line," I say. Hardly anyone uses it anyway, mainly because we've changed the number so many times that no one can keep track of it. Except, apparently, the anti-abortion psychos. I stand up and walk toward the phone, and I'm just about to yank the cord from the phone jack when the next message starts.

It's the same voice. "Hello again, baby killers," he says. "I just left a little surprise for you in the mailbox." *Click.*

I freeze.

"Don't unplug it," Dad says. "Pass me the phone. I'm calling the police."

My heart is beating fast and my hand is slippery with sweat as I hand him the phone. "It'll be okay," Mom says. "We've been here before, right?"

I nod. Last time we had a bomb threat, someone actually left a package on the front steps and we had to evacuate the house. The bomb squad came and everything, but it turned out to be just a cardboard box full of phone books and cans of hairspray.

That was over a year ago, but I still have nightmares about it.

Dad is talking to Detective Bowerbank, AKA Rich—balding,

beer-bellied and solid as a rock. Over the last few years, we've seen so much of him that he's become kind of a family friend.

I pull my cell out of my pocket. Mom grabs my arm. "Wait."

"Can't I call Leah?"

"Turn off your cell," she says. "Remember?"

Bomb threat protocol: don't touch the light switches, turn off your cell phone. I swallow and shut down my phone.

Mom tucks a wiry curl behind her ear. Her hair is a mass of tightly coiled silver springs. Like hundreds of tiny Slinkys. "Just to be on the safe side," she says. "I'm sure it'll turn out to be nothing."

Dad hangs up the phone. "He says to sit tight and they'll have someone here within a few minutes."

"Shouldn't we get out?" I ask.

"He doesn't want us opening the doors until they've made sure it's safe for us to do so."

I imagine a sniper hiding behind a tree. Picture wires trailing from the mailbox to the door hinge. My breathing is fast and shallow, and I have to remind myself to push aside the scary images. *Don't make this worse than it is, Franny.* I count silently to ten, trying to slow my breathing.

But I can't stop my thoughts. What if it's starting all over again?

Chapter Two

Half an hour later, I'm sitting with my parents in the living room, and the cops have taken away an envelope of white powder to be analyzed.

"Almost certainly not anthrax," Rich Bowerbank tells us. "Obviously, we can't take any chances, but I can tell you that out of many hundreds of similar threats to abortion clinics, none have contained actual anthrax."

"This isn't a clinic though," Mom says. "It's our house."

She is sitting on the couch beside me, her face calm, her back as straight as a dancer's. All that yoga. I straighten my own spine and lift my chin in an effort to look less like a curled-up ball of fear. "Which means someone knows where we live," I say. My voice is shaky. I clear my throat. "Do you think it's the same person as last time?"

He shakes his head. "Highly unlikely. I'll double-check, but I'm pretty sure he's still getting three meals a day at taxpayers' expense."

"He's still in jail?" I ask.

Rich nods. "Could be linked, I suppose. We'll look at every possibility." He leans toward me. "You know how seriously we take this, right?"

I nod. I do know. And Rich is a good guy. He investigated the threats at the hospital and the fake bomb at our house, and he's the one who helped bring in the guy responsible for it all. He's got daughters—twin girls, a year behind me at school—and I know he cares about our safety. And he gets it too: unlike a lot of people, he understands why my parents don't give up, even after my dad's not-quite-a-stroke.

The crazy thing is, my dad was actually just about to retire before this all started up the last time. He had high blood pressure and some other health stuff going on, and he thought less stress might be a good thing. But then all three of the doctors who did abortions at the hospital—my parents and Jennifer Lee—started getting death threats, and someone threw a brick through Jennifer Lee's dining-room window with a note attached: *NEXT TIME IT'LL BE A BULLET*.

Jennifer has a paraplegic husband and two little kids. She decided she couldn't risk it. Now she delivers babies, does some routine surgeries—but no more abortions.

So if my dad had retired too, it'd only be my mom left. And it's not just the hospital clinic here in town either. Both of them also do clinic hours each month in several smaller rural hospitals, because otherwise abortion wouldn't be available there. Sure, if you can afford to travel, you can go to a city to get an abortion. But if you're poor and live out in the sticks and don't have a car, or you have a houseful of kids to look after, or you're a sixteen-year-old whose parents don't have your back, you're screwed.

And since abortion is legal and the anti-choice people haven't had much luck getting that changed, they're going after the doctors. Trying to stop abortions by making doctors too scared to do them.

My parents don't like being bullied. I think all the threats have just made them even more committed to their work.

My dad sighs and leans back in his chair. "Rich, assuming the anthrax turns out to be baking soda, what's our next step here? Obviously, we can change our phone number, but knowing that someone has our address… I'm not sure what more we can do."

They start discussing security systems and cameras, all of which we already have. I excuse myself and clean up the dinner table, tossing the congealing pasta into a container and sticking it in the fridge. Then I head up to my room to call Leah.

My bedroom is my favorite place in our house. I repainted it myself last year, two walls white and two walls lime green. It's got a wood floor, and the rug is a dark cherry color. My parents bought me matching bedding—dark red with big geometric shapes in the exact same green as the walls. Show-jumping ribbons hang from a picture rail, and my dresser is covered with trophies. When I first invited Leah over, I was worried she'd think it was bragging to have them all out, but she totally understood. "Well, they're not really yours, right?" she said, when I started apologizing. "They're yours and Buddy's."

I have photos of Buddy all over the wall—Buddy jumping, Buddy rolling in the mud, Buddy looking out over his stall door, the white star on his forehead with a trail like a comet. I've had Buddy since I was eleven, and for the last six years he's been my best friend.

No matter what else has been going on in my life, Buddy's been there for me.

I look at the screen saver on my computer: a photo of Leah and me, both sitting bareback on Buddy as he grazes. The late-afternoon sun is shining with that golden, glowing kind of light, and the late-fall trees are bare of leaves. Buddy's coat is gleaming red chestnut, and Leah's face is turned toward the camera in an open-mouthed laugh. Jake took the photo on my phone, because I asked him to. I wanted to capture the moment, though he didn't know why. It was three months ago, end of November. Just a few minutes after Leah's and my first kiss.

I sit cross-legged on my bed, call Leah and tell her about everything that's just happened.

"Holy crap," she says.

If I wasn't so stressed, I'd laugh. Leah never swears. Not that "crap" is

17

really swearing, but Leah's the kind of girl who actually says things like "shoot" and "darn it." It's adorable. Dorky but adorable.

"I mean, you only just *left* here," she says. "All I've done is eat dinner and start my math homework, and you've been through all that? It must have been so scary."

She knows all about the fake bomb and the brick through Jennifer's window and everything. She knows about my nightmares. "What did you have for dinner?" I say.

"What did I have for dinner? Are you serious?"

"Yes. Just…just tell me something normal, okay? Distract me."

"Oh, Franny." She is quiet for a few seconds. "Okay. I finished cleaning the tack, and Jake finished his lesson with Brandy, and Mom came home from work with a carload of groceries.

Jake and I helped her make dinner. Mashed potatoes, pork chops, broccoli…"

"Sounds good," I say.

"Do you want to come over here?" she says.

"I don't know. Maybe." I picture their cozy living room, Leah's mom, Diane, marking her students' homework at the table, Jake in his room practicing his guitar or maybe playing a computer game, the horse barn visible from the window. "But it might be weird tonight, you know?"

"You mean not talking about it? With my mom there?"

"Yeah." I chew on my bottom lip. "Acting like everything is normal. When all I can think about…" My chest is tight, and my eyes sting with tears. I rub the back of my hand across them. "I just…what if…I mean…" I start crying for real. *What if someone kills my parents? What if some nut with a gun walks into the hospital and starts shooting?* I can't bring myself to say the words, but the images in my head are vivid and bloody and oh so real. My dad in his hospital greens, sprawled in the hallway with bullet holes blossoming like poppies across his chest. My mom, trying to shield a patient with her body as a stranger pulls a gun from his bag and points it at her head, and there's a loud bang and she's falling...

"Franny. FRANNY!"

"I'm here," I choke out.

"I'm coming over," she says. "On my way."

I hang up and feel a warm rush of relief at the thought of being with her. And then, almost before I've even had time to form the thought, a wave of dread slams into me with the force of a tsunami.

If my house is a target, could being with me put Leah in danger?

Chapter Three

Leah must have made an exception to her never-exceed-the-speed-limit rule, because she is at my house in less than twenty minutes. I hear her pull into the driveway, and I fly down to let her in, rushing her past my parents and the cops and up to my room.

She pulls me in for a hug and we just stand there, my head on her shoulder, breathing in the clean, sweet scent of her shampoo mingled with the smell of horses clinging to her jacket. "Poor Franny," she says.

I lift my head and look at her. "Sorry," I say, looking around for a tissue. My nose is running, and my eyes are probably all puffy and gross-looking. "Sorry I'm such a mess."

"It's okay. Don't *apologize*. I mean, no kidding you're upset. Who wouldn't be?"

"You feel okay about being here?" I ask. "I mean, not scared or unsafe or..."

She laughs. "Given that the police are right in your living room, I'm not too worried."

"What did you tell your mom?"

Leah pulls away, studying my face. "About why I was coming over? Nothing. I just said you'd had a hard day and wanted company."

"Right." I flop onto my bed, and she lies down beside me, both of us staring up at the ceiling. There's a long silence, and I wonder what she's thinking. It's weird that you can be so close to someone and not know what they're thinking. I have to bite my tongue to not ask her that all the time.

"You think I should tell her, don't you?" she says at last.

I roll onto my side and prop myself up on one elbow so I can look at her. "I didn't say that."

"You didn't have to." She sighs. "I hate keeping secrets from her. Hannah and Esther always did that, and it really upset her. She says she wants to be the kind of mom whose kids can tell her anything."

Hannah and Esther are Leah's twin sisters. They're twenty—three years younger than Jake and three years older than Leah—and they're away at college. In the Gibson family, Jake and Leah are "the good kids." They tell the truth and go to church and help out with the horses and don't keep secrets from their mom. Hannah and Esther are the rebels. The bad girls. Although I think all they really did was get drunk at a few parties and talk back to their mom. They're in their third year of degrees in commerce and tourism or something, so it's not like they're crack addicts.

"You thought your mom would have a hard time when you came out, right?" I say, treading carefully. "And that went okay."

"Yeah. I mean, it wasn't easy. She cried when I told her. She asked if I was sure, and if it was her fault or because of what happened to Dad." She makes a face. "Which was a weird thing to say, really. Have you ever heard of someone deciding she was a lesbian because

24

her father died? It doesn't even make sense."

Leah's dad died of a brain tumor when she was thirteen. Her mom, Diane, was left to raise four teenagers and run the farm while somehow holding on to a full-time teaching job. Which had to be tough. What got her through it all, she says, was her faith. There are framed Bible quotes all over the Gibson house.

"Still," I say. "You only came out a year ago. So she accepted it pretty fast." Leah's mom joined PFLAG—Parents and Friends of Lesbians and Gays. She's even spoken at her church about how their community can be more inclusive of everyone.

Leah nods. "Yeah. She got her head around it. She says there is no way that God's plan doesn't include every single one of his children. She says if this is what I am, then it's because God intended it to be that way."

I've heard this story before, but it gives me goose bumps every time. Because although I'm not religious at all, I can see that what Diane did was seriously huge. To take something you've always believed was wrong—and then, because you love your kid, turn that belief upside down? "It's impressive," I say. "You know? To support you like that, given where she started."

Leah shrugs. "Well, your parents supported you too. And you were way younger when you came out. If I'd come out at twelve, I don't think my mom would've even believed me." She blushes. "At twelve, I didn't have a clue. I was really young, you know? Still playing with dolls."

"I've always known," I say. "Always. But it wasn't a big deal for my parents. They have lots of queer friends. And it wasn't like it came as a big shock or anything." I shrugged. "I've wanted to marry my best girl friends since preschool. And I wasn't ever a very *girly* kind of girl." I run my fingers through my short hair and grin at her.

"I was," Leah says. "Pink clothes, princess obsession and all."

"You still are," I say. "I mean, maybe not the princess obsession, but yeah. *Total* girly-girl."

She laughs. Then the smile slips from her face, and her forehead creases. "My mom being so accepting about the lesbian thing…are you thinking that means she'll accept this too? What your parents do?"

"I think it shows she can be open-minded," I say. "It shows she can rethink her beliefs."

Leah shakes her head. "It's totally different. Because—"

"Why? Both have to do with thinking a certain way and then—"

She puts her fingers on my lips, shushing me. "Let me finish, okay? It's totally different, because when I came out, she had to question what she'd learned."

I nod. "Uh, yeah. I get that." Religion was a subject we mostly avoided.

"But this abortion thing," Leah said. "My mom is definitely against that. And there's no reason for her to change."

"But there is," I say, pulling away from her and up to sit cross-legged on the bed. "She likes me, right? And she knows that you…well, that you like me."

"But she hates what your parents do. Or she would if she knew." Leah shakes her head. "Seriously, Franny. It's not worth it."

"*I'm* not worth it, you mean."

I'm feeling argumentative. Maybe I'm just full of fight-or-flight chemicals after all the stress of the evening, I don't know, but I feel like I need to know that Leah's on my side. "What do you think?" I blurt out. I've never asked her this before, and as soon as the words are out of my mouth, I wish I could snatch them back.

If she sees my parents as evil baby killers, I'm not sure I want to know.

Chapter Four

Luckily, Leah misunderstands my question. "What do *I* think? I think the only reason my mom changed her mind about gay people was because I came out. Otherwise she'd still think it was wrong and a sin and all that."

"But if she met my parents...If she understood what they do and why it matters..." I trail off. "Women used to *die* because they couldn't get safe abortions. That's how my dad got into this in the first place. When he was a medical student, in the early seventies? He used to see women admitted to hospital with bleeding, infections, all kinds of awful stuff. Some of them had abortions in dirty back-alley-type places. Or they tried to give themselves abortions."

Leah interrupts. "It doesn't matter, Franny. Not to my mom. She says life begins at conception and that's that." Her blue-green eyes meet mine, wide and honest and steady. "To her, it's murder. And so it doesn't matter how you explain it. You can't justify murder."

"To her, it's murder," I repeat. In my mind, I am hearing the voice on the phone: *baby killers.*

Leah nods. "Yes. To *her*, Franny. Not to me."

I relax ever so slightly. I needed to hear that. "You don't see it that way?"

She drops her gaze. "I don't know what I think exactly. I like your parents. I know they're good people. But the way I was brought up—we were taught it was wrong."

"You were taught that being queer was wrong too," I point out.

She sighs. "I know. But abortion? I mean, I wouldn't judge anyone for doing what they think is right for them. I guess…well, it's complicated."

"*Complicated*. How is it complicated? Women have a right to control their bodies. Abortion is legal. We're getting death threats because my parents are doctors providing care to women who need it." My heart is racing. "It seems pretty obvious who the bad guys are."

"Look, there's a whole lot of things that aren't clear to me anymore. This last year…I've had to rethink a lot of what I've been taught. You know that." Leah takes both of my hands in hers.

"My mom really likes you. And she accepts us being together, which means so much to me. Can we please not wreck everything by telling her about your parents?"

I know she's right. I just don't want to accept it.

The stupid thing is, until the phone call tonight, I'd hardly even thought about Leah's views on abortion, let alone her mother's.

But if the threats and everything are going to start up all over again, I'd really like to know that my girlfriend is 100 percent on our side.

I squeeze her hands and let out a long, shaky sigh. "Okay. I mean, fine. Why rock the boat, right?"

"Exactly." She smiles, and the relief on her face is as clear and bright as sunshine. "I love you, Franny Green."

I close my eyes for a second, holding my breath, trying to hold on to this moment and keep it inside me. Then I open my eyes and she is still there, wide-eyed, waiting.

"I love you too, Leah Gibson," I say. And then I kiss her, tasting the mint of her lip gloss, and she buries her cool fingers in my short hair and pulls me down beside her on the bed

And that is the end of that conversation—of any conversation—for quite some time.

After Leah leaves, I go online and torture myself for a couple of hours reading articles about bombings at abortion clinics, receptionists and nurses being gunned down in Planned Parenthood offices, doctors shot in their own homes.

Most of the stories are from the States, but some are from as far away as Australia and a surprising number are from Canada too. Like this doctor who was shot by a sniper firing a rifle into his kitchen. The bullet hit an artery, and the doctor would have died if he hadn't used his bathrobe belt as a tourniquet. After he recovered, he kept on providing abortions. He'd seen what it was like in the sixties, before abortion was legal. He'd worked on hospital wards that were literally overflowing with women suffering complications from illegal abortions. He'd seen women die.

A few years after he was shot, he was attacked again and stabbed. And he still didn't quit. Two months later, he was back at work.

Not everyone's been so lucky, if that's even the right word. I've grown up with the stories. I know the names of those who've died: Barnett Slepian, John Britton, George Tiller, David Gunn,

Shannon Lowney, Lee Ann Nichols…so many brave men and women.

A couple of years ago someone made a website with a list of abortion providers on it. *Killers Aborted*, it was called. The doctors who'd been murdered were at the top of the page, with their names crossed out. And down at the bottom was a long list of other names—doctors still alive and doing abortions.

Including my parents.

The site's been taken down, but I still google my parents' names regularly, just to make sure they're not on some nut's hit list.

I type their names into the search bar, but all that comes up is the usual stuff—a handful of hits, mostly articles they've published, conferences they've spoken at and a ton of links about another Dr. Heather Green, who's a cosmetic surgeon. Nothing alarming.

Nothing alarming on the Internet, that is. There's still someone out there, somewhere.

Someone who knows where we live.

Chapter Five

The next day, I suffer through six hours of classes, toss my heavy bag in the backseat of my old hatchback and drive down to the barn to see Buddy.

Leah's in the stables already, waiting for me. "Buddy's looking good today," she says. "He was cantering around in the field like a yearling when I got home."

The air smells like alfalfa and molasses and saddle soap. I breathe in deeply and feel comforted. "Yeah?"

"Yeah. You want to take him out? Come with me for a gentle trail ride?" She gestures at the gray mare standing in cross ties in the aisle. "Buddy's girl-friend's hoping you'll say yes."

I laugh. "Yes. But since when did we decide our horses were straight?"

We tack up Buddy and Leah's mare, Snow, and head out. The air is cold and clear, and the frozen crust of earth on the dirt trail crunches under the horses' hooves. It feels good to be back in the saddle.

"School okay?" Leah asks as we cut off into the woods.

She's at a private Christian school. I'm at the regular public one. "Fine," I say. "Blah, blah. You know."

I don't feel like talking about school. Not that it's terrible or anything.

It's just what I have to do. I'm in my second-last year, so grades matter. I'm pretty sure I want to be a vet, and veterinary medicine is even harder to get into than med school. So I work hard, manage mostly A's and generally feel disconnected from it all.

My life—my friends, my heart, my every spare minute—has always been with the horses. From sixth grade, when I got Buddy, to last spring, when he started having trouble with his leg, I spent every evening and weekend at the hunter-jumper stables where Buddy used to board. Lessons three days a week. Setting up jumps, schooling over trot poles, hours riding without stirrups to strengthen my legs, cleaning tack and braiding manes and rubbing down horses and getting up in the middle of the night to travel to shows.

I thought the kids I rode with were my friends, but when I retired Buddy and moved him to the Gibsons', those relationships kind of fizzled out. There are a few people I still talk to occasionally, but it's not the same as when you're together all the time.

Leah and I ride on through the bare trees, mostly in silence, enjoying the stillness of the woods. Then Snow whinnies, her head lifted, and I can see the white cloud of her breath. A second later, I hear hoofbeats—someone coming down the trail at a steady lope.

"It's Jake," Leah says as a huge black horse with a red-jacketed rider appears around a bend in the trail.

Jake pulls his gelding, Schooner, up to a walk. He nods to us without smiling.

"Hi," I say, moving to the side of the trail and halting to let them pass.

"Buddy's looking good." He takes both reins in one hand and adjusts his helmet.

I can see the steam rising from Schooner's sweat-soaked chest and neck. "He's definitely better," I say. "And he's happy to be out here, for sure."

As if in agreement, Buddy tosses his head up and down, and Leah laughs.

"I have to get back," Jake says and nudges Schooner into a trot.

Leah looks at me and sighs.

I shrug. "Whatever. It's fine."

"It's not fine," she says. "He's being a jerk."

Jake and I got along really well all last summer, when I first moved Buddy to the Gibsons'. When Buddy was too lame to ride, Jake used to let me take out one of his horses, so we could ride together. And I helped with his riding lessons, setting up jumps for the kids he teaches. We weren't super close or anything—he's a lot older, for one thing—but we hung out. Not friends, but friendly.

Right up until I got together with his sister. He's barely spoken to me since he found out.

"He'll get over it, or he won't," I say. After almost three months, I'm not holding my breath. "Either way, there's nothing we can do about it."

Leah has that pink flush under her eyes that means she's trying not to cry. "I'm sorry."

"Don't apologize," I say. "You can't control what he thinks. Anyway, you're way more upset about it than I am."

She twists her fingers in Snow's long white mane. "He's my brother. You know?"

"Yeah." Though as an only child, I don't know that I can really understand. "At least Hannah and Esther are cool with us," I say.

Leah laughs. "Hannah and Esther think it's the coolest thing ever."

After we get the horses settled back in their stalls and give them a couple of flakes of hay, we head up to the house. Leah's mom, Diane, has invited me to stay for dinner.

"Pizza," she says as we walk in. "Is that okay, Franny? You eat dairy, right? And wheat?"

"I eat everything," I say. "Seriously. I don't think there is any kind of food that I don't like—except okra."

Leah makes a face. "Doesn't count as a food."

Diane laughs. "Luckily, I made my special okra-free pizza." She opens the oven door and peeks in. "Maybe five more minutes. So, can I get your advice about something?"

She sits down at the kitchen table and gestures for us to join her. She looks a little nervous—biting her bottom lip like Leah does and twisting her fingers together. Diane is ten years younger than my mom and a hundred times less confident.

"Sure," I say, curious. "What's up?"

Diane puts her elbows on the table and props her chin on her hands. "It's about a woman at my church. She approached me the other day because she'd heard about Leah. Being gay, I mean. Turns out her son has just come out to her. He's older—almost thirty, I think—but she's beside herself. She hasn't told her husband, and she's scared of how he'll react."

I roll my eyes. It's rude, I know, but I can't help it.

Diane catches my expression and smiles. "I know it must seem silly to your generation, but these people are older. In their sixties."

"So's my dad," I say. "Doesn't mean you have to be a bigot."

"Did you tell her about PFLAG?" Leah asks. "Maybe if she could meet

45

some other parents and hear their stories…"

"Of course," Diane says. "I invited her to our next meeting."

My phone rings in my pocket and I pull it out, glancing at the screen.

"Sorry," I say to Diane. "It's my mom. I should just…" I answer the phone. "Mom? What's up?"

"Oh honey," she says, and I can hear the strain in her voice. "I'm in the emergency room. It's your father."

And the air all whooshes out of my lungs like I just got kicked in the chest.

Chapter Six

"At the hospital?" I say. "What happened? Is he…is Dad…"

Leah's hand flies to her mouth, and the color drains from her face.

"So stupid," Mom says. "He was just taking out the recycling, and he slipped on the ice. Broken ankle. Badly broken, apparently. They're going to pin it."

She breaks off. "Franny, honey. Are you *crying*? What's wrong?"

"I thought…" I choke out. "For a second, I thought…" I thought he'd been shot. But I can't say it. Not in front of Diane.

"You thought he'd had a stroke?" Mom says. "No, no. Stop worrying. Your dad's as fit and strong as plenty of men twenty years younger."

"Yeah." I wipe my hand across my eyes, blinking away tears.

"Though he'll be off his ankle for six weeks. Honestly, I can't quite see how we're going to manage that. Still, one step at a time, right?"

"Right." My heart rate is slowly returning to normal. Leah and Diane are both staring at me. "Should I come to the hospital?"

"No point," she says. "You'd just be waiting around anyway. I'll stay here with him until he's out of surgery.

We'll see you at home, though probably not until the morning. Don't wait up."

"Okay," I say. "See you in the morning."

When I hang up, Diane puts her hand on my shoulder. "What is it, Franny? What happened?"

"My dad slipped on the ice," I say. "He broke his ankle."

"Oh dear." She hesitates. "I'm glad it's not worse. You looked so upset…"

I look down at the floor. "I thought… um, he has high blood pressure. And awhile back, he had a ministroke type thing." I shrug. "So I thought the worst, you know?"

None of that is technically untrue, but I still feel like I am lying to her.

"Do you want to stay the night?" she says. "If you'd rather not be at home by yourself?"

I hesitate. The front door bangs open and Jake walks in. He stands there, staring coldly at me for a moment, then pulls off his boots and walks down the hall without saying a word. I shake my head. "No," I say. "I should go home. I'll be fine."

A couple of hours later, I regret those words.

I'm not fine at all. The house is too empty, too quiet. The street outside is too dark. The park that runs along our back-yard is full of trees, any one of which could hide a sniper. I close the blinds, double-check the locks on the front and back doors and turn on all the lights.

I'm seventeen, for god's sake. It's not like I'm not used to being home alone. But I haven't been this spooked since I watched three horror movies back to back at a sleepover when I was thirteen.

I want to call Leah, but it's almost midnight. I curl up on the couch in the family room—it's at the front of the house, away from the park—and check my email and Facebook. Then I flip through the photos on my phone. Almost all of my pictures are of Leah, Buddy and other people's horses. Finally, my almost-dead battery dies, which I guess is probably a sign that I should go brush my teeth and get into bed.

Then the phone rings. The landline. And the only person who would call me this late is my mom. I jump up, run to the phone and answer it on the second ring. "Hello?"

There is an odd pause, and I know even before I hear the voice. Maybe I should just hang up, but I can't. I'm frozen to the spot.

"You'll burn in hell for what you've done." The voice is low, muffled—like he is covering his mouth or speaking into a towel to disguise his identity. "All those babies you've killed.

All those unborn children whose deaths you're responsible for."

I'm flooded with anger. And I want to know who this person is at the other end of the phone line, this person who thinks he has a right to threaten my parents. To turn our lives upside down. "Stop calling us," I say. "You're crazy."

"There's a target on your back, Heather Green," the voice says. "If you don't stop, we're prepared to use lethal force to stop you."

He thinks I'm my mom. "You're wrong about everything," I say.

"You're a mother. You should know better."

"Why are you doing this?" I demand. "Who are you?"

"Baby killer. Maybe we'll murder *your* child," he says. "Your daughter. Her name's Franny, right?"

I hang up, drop the phone and stare at it like it's a poisonous snake that might suddenly attack me. My heart is racing, my whole body shaking.

They know my name.

Then I feel stupid and embarrassed, because they've known my parents' names for years. My mom and dad live with that every single day, and they don't let it stop them.

I pick the phone back up and dial my mom's cell.

She answers right away. "Franny?"

"Mom." I'm determined not to cry, but my voice wobbles. I can't help it. "That guy called again."

"Oh, honey. Are you okay?"

"Kind of freaked out. He knew my name."

"Look, maybe you should call Rich Bowerbank."

"It's the middle of the night," I say.

"I know. But he gave us his home number…and I don't like the idea of you being there on your own."

Nor do I. "I'm going to come to the hospital," I say. "Are you in emerg?"

"In my office," she says. "Quieter place to wait. Perks of being on staff, right?"

"I'll be there in ten minutes," I say. "Maybe fifteen."

"You've got school in the morning," she protests. "You can't be up all night."

"Believe me," I say, "I'm more likely to sleep there than I am here."

Chapter Seven

But when I get to my mom's office, she's not there. I go inside, sit on her desk chair and wait. I've never in my whole life felt so completely exhausted.

I'm almost asleep, my head on my arms, when she comes back.

"Franny." She touches my shoulder lightly. "We should find you an empty bed."

I shake off the sleepiness. "Where were you? Were you with Dad? Is he out of surgery?" I notice the dark circles under her eyes. "You look worse than I feel."

"It's been a hell of a day," she says.

"Is Dad okay?"

"Fine. Doped to the gills but fine." She hesitates.

"What?"

"The call you got. Was it right before you called me?"

"Yeah. Like, literally just a few seconds before. Why?"

"Because right after I got off the phone with you, I got a page from security. The hospital received a threat and—" She breaks off at a knock on the door. "Come in."

Two cops enter. One is a man, young, black, heavyset. The other is female and about Mom's age, with short gray-blond hair and wire-framed glasses. "Dr. Green?" she says.

"Yes." My mom beckons them to take a seat. "And this is my daughter, Franny. She answered the call at our house"—she glances at her watch—"almost an hour ago."

The female cop nods, introduces herself and her partner and asks me to repeat word for word what the caller said.

I do my best. *Baby killer. You'll burn in hell. Lethal force.* The female cop, whose name I've instantly forgotten, writes it down, but it all sounds silly and melodramatic—like something on a true-crime special. But when I get to the part where he said, *There's a target on your back, Heather Green*, I break down and start crying again.

"Very upsetting," the male cop— Barnwell? Bromwell? Browning?— says. He says it kind of tersely, though, like he really just wants me to toughen up and get on with it.

He's right too. I take a deep breath, clench my fists and get on with it. "He said maybe they should kill my kid—I mean, my mother's kid. He thought I was her—and they knew my name—"

"Did he say your name? Or just claim to know it?" he asks.

"He said it. He said, *It's Franny, right?*"

My mom looks pale, and her lips are pressed together so tightly they've almost disappeared. She squeezes my shoulder but says nothing.

"And Franny, did he say *they*? Or *I*?"

"What?" I don't understand.

The female cop leans forward. "He means, did the caller refer to himself as a single person? Did he say *we should kill your kid*, or *I should kill your kid*? Try to remember. It could be important."

It's like some bizarre sentence-diagramming exercise: pronouns and verbs. The pronoun seems rather unimportant, compared with the verb *kill* and the object *me*. But I think back, trying to recall his exact words. "I think he said *we*," I say slowly. "But I'm not 100 percent sure." I meet her eyes, which are pale and blond-lashed behind the glasses. "Does it matter? I mean, couldn't he just be lying anyway? Trying to make us think he's part of a group when he's just some lone nutcase?"

"It's possible," she says. "But at this point, we want to get as much information as possible. Tell us about his voice. How did it sound? High-pitched? Low? Did he speak slowly or fast? Did he have an accent?"

"Low," I say. "Well, lowish. A man, for sure. And not fast or slow. No accent—at least, not that I noticed.

His voice was kind of muffled, like he was trying to disguise it. Speaking with something over his mouth, maybe." I try to imitate him, putting my hand over my mouth and speaking in a deep voice. "Like this." I take my hand away. "Only he didn't sound like that. Obviously."

"That's helpful, Franny," she says, making a note. "Thank you."

"What was the threat to the hospital?" I ask. "Was it a phone call?"

"Yes." She exchanges glances with the other cop, who nods, and then looks at my mother.

"You can tell her," my mom says.

"The phone call was made by a male caller." The cop leans forward, elbows on her knees. "He told us he'd left a package in one of the third-floor restrooms near the women's clinic. *A warning package*, he said." She shook her head. "We would have treated it like a bomb threat, but someone had actually found the package right before he called and opened it—stupid thing to do—"

"They *opened* it? Not staff, then," I say. "They'd know better."

"No, no. A fourteen-year-old girl who was supposed to be in bed in the pediatric ward but was in fact pissing around the hallways with her boyfriend."

I laugh, but stop quickly. It could have been very unfunny. "And it was nothing?"

"Just a box wrapped up like a gift. Inside, a doll with its arms and legs pulled off. And a note saying the next one will be a bomb." She shakes her head. "At least the kids had the sense to report it."

"You think it's the same person? The guy who called our house?"

She nods. "It seems likely. The phone call to the hospital came right around the same time as the call to your house. Right after, we think."

"So he made one phone call and then the other…" I break off. "But he must have come here first. To leave the box. So maybe someone saw him?"

"We're going to go public with this," she said. "Ask for people who were at the hospital this evening to come forward if they saw anything. Someone carrying a wrapped gift in a hospital— you wouldn't think anything of it. But if we're lucky, someone will remember and we'll get a description. If he's working alone, maybe someone saw a man going into the women's restroom."

Given the fact that I've had people freak out in women's restrooms more than once because they think I'm a guy, this seems likely. I don't even look like a guy. I'm just not as girly as most girls. As Leah—

"Wait," I say. "This'll be on the news?"

"In the morning. Yes."

"Will our names be used?" I ask.

"I made a statement," Mom says. "As department head, I thought it was important. So my name will be, at least. And I suspect the media will make the link back to the threats in the past... Jennifer Lee resigning..."

She's still talking, but I've stopped listening. All I can think about is that Diane Gibson is going to find out what my parents do after all.

I've always been so proud of my parents' work, and I *know* how important it is—but right now I wish they did almost anything else.

And I hate myself for feeling that way.

Chapter Eight

It's almost morning by the time Mom, Dad and I get home. Dad's cranky and sore, despite being medicated, and Mom's stressed, and none of us gets more than a couple of hours' sleep.

Mom says she'll write me a note if I want to stay home, but I decide to go to school. It's Friday, and I just want things to feel normal. As normal as possible anyway.

I shower, dress, force down some toast and send Leah a text: **Call me. We need to talk.**

Leah texts back almost immediately. **On school bus. What's up?**

I chew on my bottom lip. **Threats at hospital last night. Will be in news. Including my mom's name.**

You okay?

Am I okay? Good question. Not so much. **Tired. Worried about your mom seeing news.**

There's a long pause while I wait for Leah to respond. I wish I was actually talking to her. I want to hear her voice.

Finally her reply appears on the screen. **Come over after school. Better if you tell her yourself.**

I text a sad face. **Hope she doesn't freak out.**

Me too.

Love you, I type. **XO**

XXXXXXXXXXXXXXXXXXXXX
OOOOOOOOOOOOOOOOO back at you.

Hugs and kisses. I touch the screen with my finger as if I can scoop them up and hold on to them to get me through the seven hours until I see her.

School is a blur of hallway chatter and locker doors slamming and teachers' voices droning. I have to fight to stay awake. I actually doze off in my afternoon math class, head on my desk, and wake up with my cheek in a puddle of drool. Charming.

Three o'clock can't come fast enough.

Finally the bell rings and I'm free, in my car and driving to the Gibsons', windows open to let in the cold, fresh air, radio blasting. By the time I pull in to their long driveway, I'm feeling oddly optimistic.

Maybe this is a good thing, having it all come out. After all, a few days ago I was arguing that we should tell Diane. Having secrets sucks.

Besides, if Leah and I are going to stay together, eventually our parents will want to meet one another. Sooner or later we'll have to deal with this. And the more time that goes by, the harder it will be. I don't want Leah's mom to feel like I've lied to her.

I park by the barn and glance at the time on my phone. Three thirty. Leah won't get here for another fifteen minutes at least, and Diane's rarely home before four, so I head in to see Buddy. He lifts his head and whickers a greeting—or more likely a request for a treat. I keep a bag of carrots in my tack box in front of his stall door, and he knows it. It's the main reason he loves me, but I don't mind. I snap a carrot in half and hold it out to him, enjoying the warmth of his breath and the velvet softness of his lips against my palm.

"Buddy, Buddy, Buddy," I say, leaning my forehead against his and kissing his white star. "What would I do without you?"

A noise startles me—a metallic clatter—and I turn to see Jake leaning his pitchfork against the wall. He must have been mucking out stalls at the other end of the barn, but I didn't even hear him approach. He's wearing baggy coveralls and a wool hat jammed over his short blond hair.

"Hi," I say.

Jake grabs the handles of his wheelbarrow—it's full of wet wood shavings and horse manure—and walks away without a word.

"Right," I say. "Good to see you too."

Even for Jake, that was rude.

Leah comes flying into the barn a few minutes later. She's wearing a navy duffle coat and a white wool hat over her long hair, and her cheeks are pink from the cold.

I slip out of Buddy's stall and hold my arms wide, and she throws herself into them as if we haven't seen each other for days. I hold her tightly and wish we could just stay here forever.

"Leah, Leah, Leah," I murmur.

She laughs, pulls away and unbuttons her coat so that I can slip my arms around her inside it. She's wearing her school uniform—a plaid kilt, which is sexy as hell on her. It kills me that private schools still make their students dress in a uniform that is total porn-fantasy material. I mean, do they not know?

Leah kisses me, and I kiss her back, sliding my hand under her shirt to feel the warm silky skin of her lower back.

"Mmmm," she says. "I've missed you."

"Me too." There's a noise outside, and I'm so on edge that I actually startle, jumping back like a spooked horse.

"What's wrong?" she says.

"I don't know. Nervous," I say. "But we shouldn't start making out here anyway. Jake's around. He was mucking out stalls, but he didn't even say hi. Totally ignored me."

She makes a face. "Let's go up to my room. He won't bug us there."

At the sound of Diane's car door shutting and the beep of her alarm, we leap off Leah's bed, straighten out our clothes and rush down to the living room so that when she walks in, we're sitting on the couch like we've been there the whole time.

I don't know if she's fooled at all, but from the way she greets me—relaxed, friendly, normal—I guess she hasn't heard about my parents. Which is good. I'd rather she heard it from me.

"Can you stay for dinner, Franny?" she asks me. "You're very welcome."

"Thanks," I say. "If it's no trouble. I feel like you're always feeding me."

She smiles. "I like feeding people. And I'm used to having lots of hungry mouths to feed. With Esther and Hannah gone, the house feels so quiet and empty."

"You should see my house sometime," I say. "Quiet and empty is normal for me. But thanks. Can I help?"

"You and Leah can make a salad," she says. "I'm just reheating some soup

71

from the freezer, and there's some corn bread a friend made."

"Perfect," I say. The first few times I ate dinner here, Diane made a big fuss—cooking up these complicated meals. Leah said it was her mom's way of letting me know she was okay with Leah and me being together, but I'm glad she's relaxed enough now to feed me reheated soup. It makes me feel more like part of the family.

Leah pulls lettuce and assorted vegetables out of the fridge, and I start washing and chopping while I wonder how on earth I am going to bring up the subject of my parents. I can't just blurt it out—*oh, by the way, my parents are abortion providers*—but there's no obvious way to lead into the subject. I look sideways at Leah, who is dicing avocado, and mouth, *Now what?*

She just gives me a deer-in-the-headlights stare and shrugs helplessly.

Diane is standing at the stove, stirring the soup, which smells really spicy and good. She glances over at us. "You look a little pale, Franny. Are you okay?"

"Just super tired," I say. "Um, last night? I was at the hospital and—"

"Of course," she says. "Your father. How is his ankle?"

"He has to stay off it for a while," I say. "But, uh, there was a…my parents… um…"

She waits, holding my gaze. The look on her face—steady, patient—is the exact same look I often see on Leah's face. Right down to the blue-green eyes and the head tilt. It's a little freaky how alike they are. I take a deep breath.

"One of the things they do at the hospital is abortions," I say. "And this week we've been getting some threats."

Diane looks shocked, but I can't tell whether she's shocked by what my parents do or by the fact that someone is threatening them. "He called our house," I say. "Last night."

"Oh no," she says. "You poor dear. You were home alone, weren't you? You should have stayed here…"

"So I went to the hospital." I plow on, just wanting to get this all over with now that I've started. "And he'd called there too and said he'd left a package in a restroom."

Her eyes widen. "A package? Like… not a *bomb*?"

"A warning," I say. "To show us he's serious. Next time it'll be a real bomb, he said."

"Oh, Franny." Diane turns off the stove element. "You poor thing. How scary."

"It'll be in the news," I say. "Because they're trying to find who did it."

Leah tips a heap of sliced avocado and red pepper into the salad bowl and carries it over to the table. "Franny thought you might hear about it," she says. "And she wanted to tell you herself."

I swallow. "I know I just said my parents were doctors. I don't usually get into what they do because—well, because people have different feelings about it, and it's no one's business anyway. But I didn't want you to feel like I was hiding things from you."

Diane takes four bowls from the cupboard and puts them on the table. "I appreciate your telling me," she says.

"Telling you what?" Jake says from the doorway.

"Nothing," Leah says.

Diane ladles soup into the bowls. "Sit down, all of you. Let's eat."

We sit, and Diane says a quick grace. From across the table, Jake's gaze locks onto mine, his jaw tight and eyes narrowed, and I wonder how much of our conversation he heard.

Maybe Diane's reaction wasn't the one I should've been worried about.

Chapter Nine

"So what were you all talking about?" Jake asks, heaping salad onto his plate.

I guess he's going to hear anyway. "My parents have been getting harassed," I say. "Phone calls at home, making threats. And last night someone called the hospital—"

"Why would someone do that?" Jake asks.

"Anti-abortion terrorists," I say. I refuse to call them pro-life because they're not. If anyone is for *life*, it's my parents and the nurses at the clinic, saving women's lives every day. The person who's threatening to kill us? Yeah, he's not so much about life at all.

Jake raises his eyebrows. "Calling them terrorists is a bit extreme, isn't it?"

"Um, threatening to kill people and leaving bombs in hospital restrooms *is* extreme." I put down my fork. "Anyway, what's the definition of a terrorist? Someone targeting innocent civilians and using terror to accomplish a political goal? Check."

"Your parents aren't exactly innocent though," he says. "Not if they're doing abortions."

"Jake," Diane says, a note of warning in her voice. "Let's change the subject."

Jake turns to her. "You can't be okay with this, Mom. You can't support this."

She sighs. "Jake. Please. Just drop it. My personal views are beside the point. Franny is our guest and—"

"Because she's lied to us," he snaps. "We've been taking money from them, Mom. Her horse's board has been paid for by them, with money they made killing babies. You don't have a problem with that?"

"Shut up, Jake," Leah says. "Just shut up. You don't know anything about it. You're just saying that because it's how Dad used to think."

I stand up, my heart beating so hard I think it might explode. Diane grabs my arm.

"Sit down, Franny. And Jake, you should be ashamed of yourself."

"But you—" he starts.

Diane cuts him off. "I may not agree with abortion, but I certainly don't think Franny's parents or anyone else should be in danger because of what they do."

"But Mom, they—"

"Enough, Jake. That is *enough.*" Diane raises her voice. "Go to your room. Now."

Jake doesn't move. He just laughs. "I'm twenty-three, Mom. You can't give me time-outs."

"I'm leaving anyway," I say. The room, their three faces—it's all a blur through the tears in my eyes. Tears of anger. If I don't leave, I'll hit him. I've never in my life wanted to hit someone like I do right now.

Diane stands up to. She looks like she is about to cry. "Please excuse my son's rudeness," she says. "I am so, so sorry."

Leah gets to her feet. "Oh, Franny… I'm coming with you."

"No," I say. "You're not."

I can't get out of there fast enough. I run down the driveway, fumble with my keys, get into my car and floor it. I can barely see through my tears, and I know I shouldn't be driving right now, but I don't care.

I just want to be back in my own house.

A couple of hours after I get home, Mom calls up, "Franny? Leah's here."

I open my bedroom door and yell down the stairs, "Come on up."

I can hear the low murmur of Mom and Leah talking and then Leah's footsteps on the stairs. I flop back down on my bed and wait.

Leah slips into my room and closes the door behind her. "You haven't told them? Your parents?"

"What, that your brother thinks they're murderers? No, I didn't think they really needed to hear that right now." None of this is her fault, but I feel angry with her anyway. I wish she hadn't come over.

"I don't blame you for being upset," she says carefully.

"Oh, that's generous of you."

She flinches. "Franny. I can't help what my brother thinks, okay? I don't agree with him. You know that. And I don't know if he even agrees with the stuff he's saying himself. He's just mad because he doesn't like me being with you, so he's spouting the kind of stuff Dad used to say."

I sit up. "The *kind of stuff* he's saying is the *kind of stuff* that gets people like my parents killed."

She shakes her head. "It's just words. He'd never—"

"Just words? JUST WORDS?"

"Shhh," she says. "Your parents will hear."

"You don't get it," I tell her.

"I get it," she says. "My brother is a jerk. I don't blame you for being mad.

But don't take it out on me." Her eyes shine with tears.

"There's no such thing as *just words*," I say. "Seriously. Saying that my parents murder babies? That kind of language is what makes people do crazy stuff."

"Only if they're already crazy."

I snort. "There's no shortage of crazy out there."

"I know," Leah says. She reaches out to me, runs her fingers over my eyebrows and cups my face in her hands. "It's scary. But my mom was okay, right? She didn't freak out."

"No. Jake kind of took care of the freaking-out side of things."

"I know. I'm really sorry." She bites her bottom lip. "He'll get over it."

"I'm not so sure I will," I say.

"You don't have to." Leah kisses my forehead, my nose, my lips. "As long as you still love me, even though my brother's a pain in the you-know-what." She hesitates, pulls back and studies my face. "You do, don't you?"

I laugh. "I do. Even though you can't even say *butt*."

But after she leaves, Jake's words still echo in my mind. *Killing babies. Murdering babies.*

I can't stop thinking about it. Something feels…off, somehow. I replay the conversation at the Gibsons' dinner table and realize what it is. Jake didn't seem in the least surprised about my parents being abortion providers.

Maybe he'd overheard me telling Diane.

Or maybe he already knew.

Maybe that's the real reason he's been so cold to me. Maybe it isn't just about me being involved with his sister.

And then I remember that low, muffled voice on the phone. Those same words. *Baby killers.*

What if it isn't just a coincidence?

Chapter Ten

The next day is Saturday, and despite my nervousness about seeing Jake, I spend the morning at the barn as usual. I groom Buddy, muck out his stall and clean my saddle. Jake is teaching in the arena, so it's easy to stay out of his way. I'm helping one of his students—a tiny girl with long black braids—find the right bridle for the pony she'll be riding, when Leah walks in.

"Hey," she says. "Here you go." She hands me a mug of coffee.

I send Black Pigtails on her way and take the coffee, wrapping my cold hands around it and enjoying the warmth. "Thanks. What are you up to?" I ask.

"Homework." She makes a face. "Boring. Are you going to ride?"

"Yeah." I notice that she's dressed for riding, in an old pair of beige breeches and riding boots. "Want to join me?"

"Sure. I need a break, and Snow needs exercise."

I pull my gray leather chaps out of my tack box and zip them over my jeans. "Let's do it."

But I can't stop thinking about Jake. Can't stop thinking *what if, what if, what if*. We've only gone half a mile or so when I make up my mind. I pull Buddy to a halt and jump off quickly, running my hand over his fetlock. "It's not warm or swollen or anything," I say. "But he's definitely sore. I'm going to walk him back."

Leah gives me a sympathetic look. "That sucks. I'll see you back there, then?"

"Yeah." I wave to Leah and lead Buddy back toward the barn. "Buddy, Buddy, Buddy," I say, stroking his shoulder. "Sorry about your trail ride, pal. I bet you're wondering what the hell is wrong with me, huh?"

Back in Buddy's stall, I take off his saddle and bridle and give him a quick brush-down. I can hear Jake's voice from the arena, calling out instructions to his eleven-o'clock class. "Ashley, more legs!

Don't let him be lazy. Keep those gentle hands just like that, Jude. Nice transition there, Matt! Kaylie, your leg position's looking good, but let's see a little more weight in your heels…"

He's a good teacher. Patient with the kids, gentle with the horses.

It's hard to fit the way he treats me—and the things he said about my parents—together with this other, kinder side of him.

When I listen to him with his students, I think there's no way he could be the anonymous caller. I'm being paranoid. I wish I could talk to Leah—share my suspicions with her—but it's a bad idea. She's blindly loyal when it comes to family. We'd end up fighting.

I can't believe I just lied to her. That I pretended Buddy was limping. I feel slightly sick thinking about it.

But what if it *is* Jake? What if I ignore my suspicions and something happens to my parents? How do I live with that?

I look up the driveway at the Gibsons' house. Diane's car isn't there, so she must be out.

Leah's riding Snow.

Jake's teaching…

My breath catches in my throat at the thought of what I'm about to do.

The front door is unlocked. I let myself in. "Diane?" I call out, just in case.

No one answers. I tug my boots off and pad down the hall, my heart racing. Leah's bedroom and her mom's are both upstairs, but Jake's is on the main floor. His door is closed, and as I push it open, it creaks loudly and I practically jump out of my skin.

Chill, I tell myself, Jake's lesson goes for another twenty minutes, Leah's off in the woods somewhere, and if

Diane comes home, I'll hear her car and make up some excuse for being here.

I slip into Jake's room. Narrow bed against one wall, desk with computer on it, a tidy bookshelf, guitar leaning against the wall, music stand…I scan the books on the shelves—a few old math texts, some books on HTML programming, a stack of music magazines. Biographies of musicians. Some thrillers and mystery novels—Stephen King, John Grisham, that kind of thing. No *Dummies Guide to Bombs* or anything of that sort. No Bible with conveniently marked passages. No books about the evils of abortion.

I don't know what I expected to find.

I'm turning to leave when I notice a roll of wrapping paper in the corner behind the door. Birthday theme—cake and candles.

Of course, he could just be going to a party.

On the other hand? Two nights ago, someone delivered a gift-wrapped bomb threat to the hospital.

I tear off a corner of the paper and stuff it into the back pocket of my jeans. Then I leave Jake's room, close the door behind me and sprint back down the driveway to the barn.

Jake is still teaching. I check my watch—five minutes until the lesson ends. I slide open Buddy's stall door and lean my head against him. He ignores me, contentedly munching on his hay. "What should I do, Buddy?" I whisper. "Should I talk to Leah? Or is that a really bad idea?"

He lifts his head and looks at me, blowing out a long breath through fluttering nostrils.

"Yeah," I say. "You're probably right."

I can't just ignore my suspicions. But suspicions are all I have.

And wrapping paper, which is hardly evidence of a crime. Just because Jake's anti-choice—and an obnoxious, ignorant jerk—it doesn't mean he's done anything illegal.

I know what Leah would say. I can hear her voice in my head already: *No way. Jake wouldn't do anything like that.*

I decide to leave it to fate. I'll take Buddy out to the paddock so he can spend the afternoon outside, and then I'll head home. If Leah gets back with Snow before I leave, I'll talk to her. If not…I'll let it go.

I clip a lead rope onto Buddy's halter. "Come on, Bud. Let's get out of here before Jake shows up, hey?"

I lead him outside, turn him loose in the fenced-off end of the field and return to the barn just as Jake's students are filing out of the arena. Horseshoes clatter against concrete floor, girls' voices chatter, and Jake laughs.

I hang my lead rope over Buddy's stall door, not taking the time to put it away properly, and hightail it to my car.

Guess I'm not talking to Leah.

Chapter Eleven

I spend the afternoon napping, doing homework and listening to podcasts. Dad orders takeout for dinner, and my parents and I sit around the living room together, eating Thai food and watching Netflix. Everything feels wonderfully normal. Detective Bowerbank calls to confirm that the white powder in the mailbox was not anthrax, and we celebrate by defrosting a chocolate cheesecake in the microwave and eating an impressive amount of it.

Dad finishes his second slice and pushes his plate away with a sigh. "Pad Thai, beer and cheesecake. Life is good."

Mom licks her fork. "Back on the wagon in the morning."

"I'll make dinner tomorrow," I say. "I've found this great website called Homemade and Heart Healthy—"

Dad groans and folds his hands across his belly. "Don't talk about food. I'll never be hungry again."

"Not until at least midnight," Mom says.

My cell rings. I hesitate.

"Go ahead," Dad says. "Talk to your girlfriend. You've put in your time with the old fogy."

"Dad! You're not—"

He laughs. "I meant your mother."

She pokes him with her fork. "Remind me again why I put up with you?"

I roll my eyes and answer my phone, walking toward my room. "Leah?"

"Yeah. Hi."

"Everything okay?"

"Sure. Why wouldn't it be?"

Because I snuck into your house and searched your brother's room. "No reason," I say, trying to keep my voice light. "How was your ride?"

"Good. How come you didn't wait for me to get back?"

"Take a wild guess," I say.

"Jake?"

"Yeah."

"Did he say something to you? I asked him, but he said he didn't even see you."

I clear my throat. "I'm kind of avoiding him."

"Well, you can't keep that up forever," Leah says.

I stick my hand into my jeans pocket and pull out the piece of wrapping paper. "Yeah, I know." I clear my throat. "So what are you guys up to tonight? Got a party to go to?"

"A party?" There's a pause. "No. Why?"

"I don't know. Saturday night. I just thought you might have plans. Or Jake might."

"No plans," she says. "Franny, are you okay?"

I can hear the frown in her voice. "Yeah," I say. "Yeah. I'm fine."

"Good. Want me to come over?"

Of course I want her to come over—but there's something else I have to do. "I think I'm just going to crash early tonight," I say. "I'm kind of tired."

"Oh. Okay. Sure." She sounds hurt.

"I'll be down in the morning though," I offer. "I'll see you then. When you get back from church."

And I'll see Jake, I think. She's right. I can't avoid him forever.

After we hang up, I go online and google Jake Gibson. I try Jacob Gibson too, since presumably that's what Jake is short for. I even try Jackson Gibson, though it sounds awful and doesn't fit the biblical naming scheme of Leah's family.

Nothing.

Well, not *nothing*. There are tons of Jake Gibsons—TV producers, actors, lawyers, football players. But for the Jake Gibson I'm interested in, the only things that show up are a couple of local newspaper articles about a summer riding camp he runs, his dad's obituary and some track-and-field results from back in high school. He has a Facebook page too, but his privacy settings won't let me see anything, and given that I've never seen him comment on any of Leah's posts, I'm guessing he doesn't use it much anyway.

So much for that.

I smooth out the scrap of wrapping paper and tuck it under the corner of my keyboard. Then I search for articles about the recent bomb threat at the hospital. There are several, but they're all pretty much the same—the few facts the police released, a request for the public to come forward with any information, and a rehashing of the threats from last year and Jennifer Lee's resignation. I bet she wishes they'd stop printing her name.

A gift-wrapped package was found...

No convenient detailed description of the wrapping paper.

I shake my head. I'm being crazy. Jake's just a jerk, like plenty of other people. He's anti-choice and he doesn't like me dating his sister. Which is a drag, but it's also not a huge deal. And it definitely doesn't make him a murderous lunatic. I crumple up the piece of paper and toss it in the recycling bin under my desk.

Enough craziness.

I wake up smiling the next morning. The sun is streaming through my bedroom window, and I've been dreaming about Leah.

I sit up, stretch and yawn widely.

Today is going to be a good day. I can feel it.

I dress quickly, bolt down a huge bowl of granola and nuts and yogurt, and head to the barn. No one's there—it's Sunday morning, and they're all at church. I groom Buddy till his coat shines and take him for a ride in the woods—a good long one to make up for yesterday's getting cut short. The sun streams through the bare branches of the trees, and the air has that cold, crisp feeling of fall. Buddy acts like a two-year-old, tossing his head and snorting and taking big sideways leaps of alarm over every harmless shadow and fallen twig.

"You big baby," I say, feeling a flood of affection for him.

I hear someone approaching, and Leah appears around a bend in the trail, riding bareback on her gray mare. "Franny," she says, out of breath. "I was hoping I'd find you guys. How's Buddy? Better, I guess, or you wouldn't be riding."

"He's fine today," I say. My ears feel hot at the memory of yesterday's lie.

"Good." She brings her horse alongside mine. "Mom and Jake are off looking at some old equipment on a friend's farm and won't be back till dinnertime. Got plans for the rest of the day?"

"Uh, yeah. I do now," I say, giving her a goofy grin.

Leah grins back. And my perfect morning is followed by an even more perfect afternoon.

The next day, everything falls apart.

I get home from school to find Detective Bowerbank in the living room, sitting on the couch beside my mother. "What happened?" I say, my heart in my throat. "Where's Dad? Is he okay?"

"It's fine," Mom says. "Dad's fine. He's at work. There's a security meeting."

I look at Rich. "A security meeting. Something happened? What's going on?"

He leans back on the couch, folds his arms across his belly and sighs. "Hello, Franny."

"Hello, Rich," I say. "Don't torture me. Something happened, right?"

He nodded. "Your mother received a letter at work. A threat."

"What did it say?"

He slides a page to me across the coffee table. "This is a copy. We're having the original checked for fingerprints, DNA—anything."

I stare at it. It's not a letter. It's a photograph.

My hand flies to my mouth as if I can catch the breath that has suddenly whooshed from my lungs.

"Franny," Rich says. "I know this is upsetting, but try not to worry. We're looking into this. We're going to put some extra security measures in place—"

I touch the photo. It's of my house. My parents, on our driveway.

With bright-red Sharpie targets drawn on their chests.

"Franny, wait!" Mom says, getting to her feet.

I run up to my room, throw myself on my bed and lie there, curled up in a ball.

A minute later Mom knocks on the door. "Franny? Can I come in?"

I don't answer, but she lets herself in anyway and sits on the edge of my bed. "It's horrible, I know. Scary." She rubs my back, moving her hand in slow circles. "But we've been living with this risk for years. It's going to be fine."

"You don't know that," I choke out. "You can't promise that."

Her hand stops moving. "I can't promise it," she says, "but I do believe it. So does your dad. And so does Rich. He's looking into everything, you know. Interviewing people, following up every possible lead…"

Except Jake Gibson, I think.

If I tell him about Jake, I might lose Leah.

But if I don't tell him…

If I don't tell him and it turns out that I'm right…

Then I might lose my parents.

Chapter Twelve

Leah sends me texts all evening, but I ignore them. I can't imagine telling her what I'm thinking. And I can't imagine talking to her and *not* telling her.

Late that night, I phone Detective Bowerbank. I don't want to have to talk to him in person, so I call his office phone and leave a message. I tell him about Jake and how he's been acting toward me and what he said about my parents being baby killers. I tell him that it's probably nothing and that I'm probably being stupid and that I'm sorry I'm wasting his time.

I don't mention the wrapping paper, because I don't want to admit to snooping in Jake's room, and besides, who doesn't have wrapping paper?

My message is a garbled mess, and I wish I could just erase it and start over. After I hang up, I lie on my bed and stare at the ceiling.

I can't stand the thought of losing Leah, but I don't think I could survive if something happened to my parents.

In the morning my parents head to work, and I go off to school like everything is normal.

Only it isn't.

I feel sick to my stomach all morning. I send Leah a text at lunchtime. **Miss you.**

She replies a couple of minutes later. **Miss you too. How come you weren't at the barn last night? I called you 100 times.**

So nothing's happened yet, obviously. And maybe nothing will. Maybe Detective Bowerbank will listen to my message, laugh a little about how crazy I'm being and press *Delete*. I hope he does.

I'll be there after school today, I text.

Her reply is instant. **YAY! XO**

XXXXXXXXXXXXOOOOOOOOOO, I send back.

I want every one of those in person.

I picture Leah's wide eyes, her full lips, the way the corners of her mouth lift and her cheeks dimple when she smiles. **Me too,** I tell her.

I have Biology after lunch, which I usually like, but today I spend the class thinking about Leah and hoping desperately that she'll still feel the same way about me at four o'clock. That nothing will have changed.

My lab partner elbows me. "What's wrong with you today?" She gestures at the half-dissected cow eyeball in front of us. "I thought you'd be in future-vet heaven, but you're like... somewhere else."

"Sorry," I say. The eyeball blurs and I blink back tears. "Back in a minute."

I dash to the girls' washroom, which, luckily, is empty, and dial Rich Bowerbank's number. Voice mail. "Hi, it's Franny," I say. "Listen, about that message I left last night. Just ignore it, okay? I was just freaked out about the threats and being paranoid. I mean, lots of people aren't comfortable with abortion, and it doesn't make them deranged losers. Or, you know, stalkers or murderers or whatever. So, uh, what I said about Jake? Just pretend that never happened. Um. Sorry." I hang up before I can ramble anymore.

He'll probably think I'm the one who's a deranged loser.

That's fine with me.

After school I head straight to the Gibsons'. I think at first that the barn is empty—the lights are off. I switch them on—

And see Leah, sitting on the tack box in front of Buddy's stall. Her arms are crossed, and her mouth is a thin, straight line.

"You're home early," I say stupidly. Like that's the point.

"Because Jake called me," she says. "Because the cops were here. Interviewing him…" She starts crying. "Franny, how could you?"

I shrug helplessly and stand there, just inside the barn door. Twenty feet away from her, and it feels like a mile.

"They searched his room," she says.

"Don't they need, you know, a warrant or something to do that?"

"He said they could," Leah says coldly. "He told them to look around. Let them look through his emails too."

"He did?"

"Yeah. Because he has nothing to hide, Franny. Because he hasn't *done* anything."

I slide down the wall so that I'm sitting on the cold cement floor. "I'm sorry, Leah. I'm so sorry. But—"

She cuts me off. "He didn't even know what your parents did until he heard you telling my mom the other night."

"Let me explain," I say. "Please."

"Fine. Explain." Her voice is like ice.

"There was another threat," I say. "Yesterday. A photo of my parents leaving our house, and targets were drawn on their chests...and I was so scared that something might happen to them. And Jake...the things he said..."

"You should have talked to me, Franny. I could have told you he'd never do anything like that."

"He's your brother," I say. "You trust him. Of course you wouldn't think he'd—"

"Yeah, he's my brother. I trust him because I *know* him." She meets my eyes for a second and then looks away. "And I thought you trusted me."

"I do," I say. "Of course I do."

"If you trusted me, you'd have talked to me. Not acted like everything was fine and then gone behind my back and told the police that Jake might be some crazy killer."

"I couldn't risk not saying anything to the police," I say. "Because if I didn't…if I just said nothing and if you were wrong about Jake…and if something happened to my parents…then it'd be my fault."

We stare at each other in silence for a long moment. I can't see a way forward. Can't see a way out of this.

And there's no going back.

Leah stands up. "I'm going up to the house," she says.

It's over, I think. She'll never speak to me again. She hates me, and Jake hates me, and their mother will hate me as soon as she hears about what I've done.

I'll have to move Buddy to some other stable.

Then the door swings open behind me, and I scramble to my feet.

It's Jake.

Chapter Thirteen

"I can't believe you have the balls to show up here after what you did," Jake says. "Telling the cops lies about me. Telling them—"

"I didn't lie," I say.

"Right. That's why they were here this afternoon, going through my room, asking questions about where I've been."

"All I said was that you called my parents baby killers," I say. My voice is louder than I mean it to be. "Which is *not* a lie!"

"No law against calling it like it is," Jake says. His fists are clenched. "You're crazy. A crazy dyke."

I flinch. For a moment, I wonder if he might hit me.

"Jake," Leah says. "Don't…don't use that word. Not like that."

"Stay away from us," he says. "Stay away from my sister."

I look at Leah. Her face is white, her eyes wide and shining with tears. "I'm sorry," I tell her. "I never meant to hurt you."

"Just go," she says. "Please. Just go."

I've lost her. Leah's the best thing that's ever happened to me, and it's over. It's my fault, and there's absolutely nothing I can do. I feel empty. Hollow. Every part of me aches.

I turn to leave.

And my phone rings. I hesitate, but I can't ignore it. Because the first thing that comes to mind is my parents. I take a few steps away from Jake and Leah and answer the call. "Hello?"

"Franny? It's Rich Bowerbank."

My heart thuds painfully in my chest. "What is it? Is something…has something…my parents?"

"Your parents are fine," he says quickly. "But there's been an incident."

"An incident? At the hospital?" I glance at Jake and Leah. They're both staring at me. Jake still looks angry, his fists clenched at his sides, his jaw tight. Leah's mouth is open, her fingers pressed against it. "What happened?"

"Everyone is fine," he says again. "A man came into the clinic. He pulled a knife and—"

My knees turn to jelly, and I sit down abruptly on a bale of hay. "A knife?"

"Oh my god," Leah says. "What's happened?"

I ignore her. Turn away slightly, pressing the phone to my ear.

"He was disarmed very quickly by security," Detective Bowerbank says. "We have him in custody. We're still investigating, but it looks like he's responsible for all of the threats. The phone calls, the letters…"

I start sobbing. Relief, I guess. I feel like an idiot, but I can't help it.

Leah is at my side, her face wet with tears. "Franny? Franny, your parents? Are they…has something—"

"They're okay," I say. I can hardly breathe.

"What happened?"

I end the call and stick the phone back in my pocket. "Someone showed up at the clinic," I say. My voice sounds strange. "With a knife."

"Holy crap," Jake says. He sounds kind of stunned.

I whirl on him. "You thought I was making this up or something? Making a fuss about nothing?"

"Not exactly," he says. "But—"

"Doctors get *killed*," I say. "For taking care of patients. For doing a procedure that, regardless of what *you* think about it, is legal and safe." I glare at him. "At least, safe for the patient."

He sticks his hands in his pockets. "Well, at least now you know it wasn't me."

He's right. Which means I ruined my relationship with Leah for nothing. Because I'm an idiot.

I turn and walk away. I'm half-hoping Leah will stop me—come running after me—but she doesn't.

She just stands there beside Jake and watches me leave.

My parents are both in the kitchen when I get home. Mom's grating cheese; Dad's stretching out a lump of dough.

"Hello there, Franster," Dad says. "You're home early. Buddy okay?"

"Fine." I burst into tears.

They both stare at me. "What is it?" Mom asks, sounding alarmed. "Rich said he spoke to you. They arrested the guy, Fran. It's all over."

I shake my head. Dad leaves his pizza dough on the baking tray and puts his arms around me. "Come here, Franny-bear. It's okay."

I'm crying in great heaving sobs. "Sorry," I say. "Sorry."

He just holds me, my face against his chest.

I sniff, pull back and wipe my nose on my sleeve. "I'm probably getting snot all over your sweater."

"No worries," he says. "I've got pizza dough all over yours."

I laugh through my tears.

"Franny?" Mom says. "Did something happen? Or…"

"Me and Leah," I say. "I think maybe we just broke up."

After I explain everything that happened—the things Jake said, how I snooped around his room, what I told Detective Bowerbank—Mom looks as if she might start crying herself.

"You poor kid," she says. "Your dad and I—well, you know why we do what we do. Why it's important. But we didn't want all this to affect you."

"Seriously?" I roll my eyes. "How could it not, Mom?"

"I know, I know. But…" She shakes her head. "I wish you'd talked to us."

"You had enough to worry about."

Dad has returned to his pizza, stretching the dough, spreading pesto sauce on it and slicing mushrooms as we talk. "So are you going to apologize to him?"

I stare at him. "To Jake? You've got to be kidding."

He shrugs. "Well, you did suspect him of doing some terrible things."

"Because he *said* some terrible things," I say. "He's the one who should apologize."

Dad just sighs and shakes his head.

Chapter Fourteen

I'm undressed and crawling into bed when my phone rings. *Leah.*

"Hello?" I say.

"Hi. Uh, it's Jake.

I sit up, my heart instantly racing. "Jake?"

"Don't hang up."

"I wasn't going to," I say. "What is it?"

"Look. Uh, I just wanted to say sorry that I flipped out about you telling the cops about me."

I don't say anything for a few seconds. When I told Dad I thought Jake should apologize, I never in a million years thought he actually would.

"I get why you did it," he says. "If I thought my mom was in danger, I'd probably have done the same thing."

"Yeah." I pull the covers up around my bare shoulders, shivering in the cold air. "I knew I was probably being crazy and paranoid, but—"

"You couldn't risk not saying anything," he says. "In case you were right."

"Exactly."

"Anyway," he says, "that's all I wanted to say."

I think of what my dad said. "Um. I'm sorry too. That I suspected you of doing that stuff."

He clears his throat. "I think it's wrong. Abortion, I mean. But that guy showing up with a knife…that's really twisted. Like, that's way more wrong. It kind of freaked me out, actually. That someone would do that."

I can't make sense of Jake. I can't figure out how the nice guy fits together with the guy who called my parents murderers. The guy who called me a crazy dyke. "Did you tell Leah?" I say. "That you understand why I told the police?"

"Nah."

"I know you don't like us being together," I say. "But…would you tell her? Please?"

"I haven't told her because she won't speak to me." There's a pause. "She's been in her room crying her eyes out all night."

"I never meant to hurt her."

"Yeah, well. Me neither."

"It's not the same," I say. "She'll always be your sister. But I've wrecked the best relationship I've ever had."

"I wouldn't be so sure."

"Seriously? You think she might still…"

"Leah is the most loyal person I've ever known. That's why she defended me." Jake sighs into the phone. "And that, unfortunately, probably means she's not done with you."

I don't hear from Leah that night.

Or the next day. I pick up my phone every hour or so, think about sending her a text, then put it back in my pocket.

I'm not sure if I'm just giving her space or if I'm scared to find out how she feels. Uncertainty sucks—but maybe it's better than knowing for sure that it's over between us.

After school I drive down to the Gibsons'. Buddy still needs me, even if Leah doesn't.

I park my car, looking at the long line of trees that overhang the driveway and, behind them, the horses in the field. Buddy's out there, grazing beside Snow, his blue blanket muddy from rolling on the rain-sodden ground.

I'll have to move him somewhere else, I guess. Another stable.

Then the barn door opens and Leah steps out.

"You're home already?" Then I notice she's wearing jeans and a hoodie, not her uniform. "I skipped school today," she says. "I needed to think."

I take a deep breath.

Wait.

Hope…

"I needed to think about us," she says.

"Us?" I say. "You and me?"

Leah steps toward me. Holds out her hands. Smiles in that way that lifts the corners of her lips and leaves deep dimples in her cheeks. "Yes," she says. "You and me."

Acknowledgments

Thanks as always to my wonderful and endlessly supportive family. Thanks also to Alex Van Tol for coming up with the title, and to the fabulous team at Orca Book Publishers.

Robin Stevenson is the award-winning author of numerous books for kids and teens. *Under Threat* is her fifth book in the Orca Soundings series, following *Big Guy, In the Woods, Outback* and *Damage*. Her other novels for teens include *The World Without Us, Hummingbird Heart, Escape Velocity, Inferno*, and the Governor Generals Literary Award finalist *A Thousand Shades of Blue*. Robin lives in Victoria, BC.

Titles in the Series

orca soundings

orca soundings

For more information on all the books
in the Orca Soundings series, please visit
www.orcabook.com.